Peggy Piggle's First Day of School

Created by Alexander Janda
Illustrated by Eugene Kral

All rights reserved.
Published by Xander Enterprises, Inc.
Copyright © 2024 by Alexander Janda
Peggy Piggle and Pals™ is a trademark owned by Alexander Janda
www.peggypiggleandpals.com
ISBN 978-1-7389802-0-8

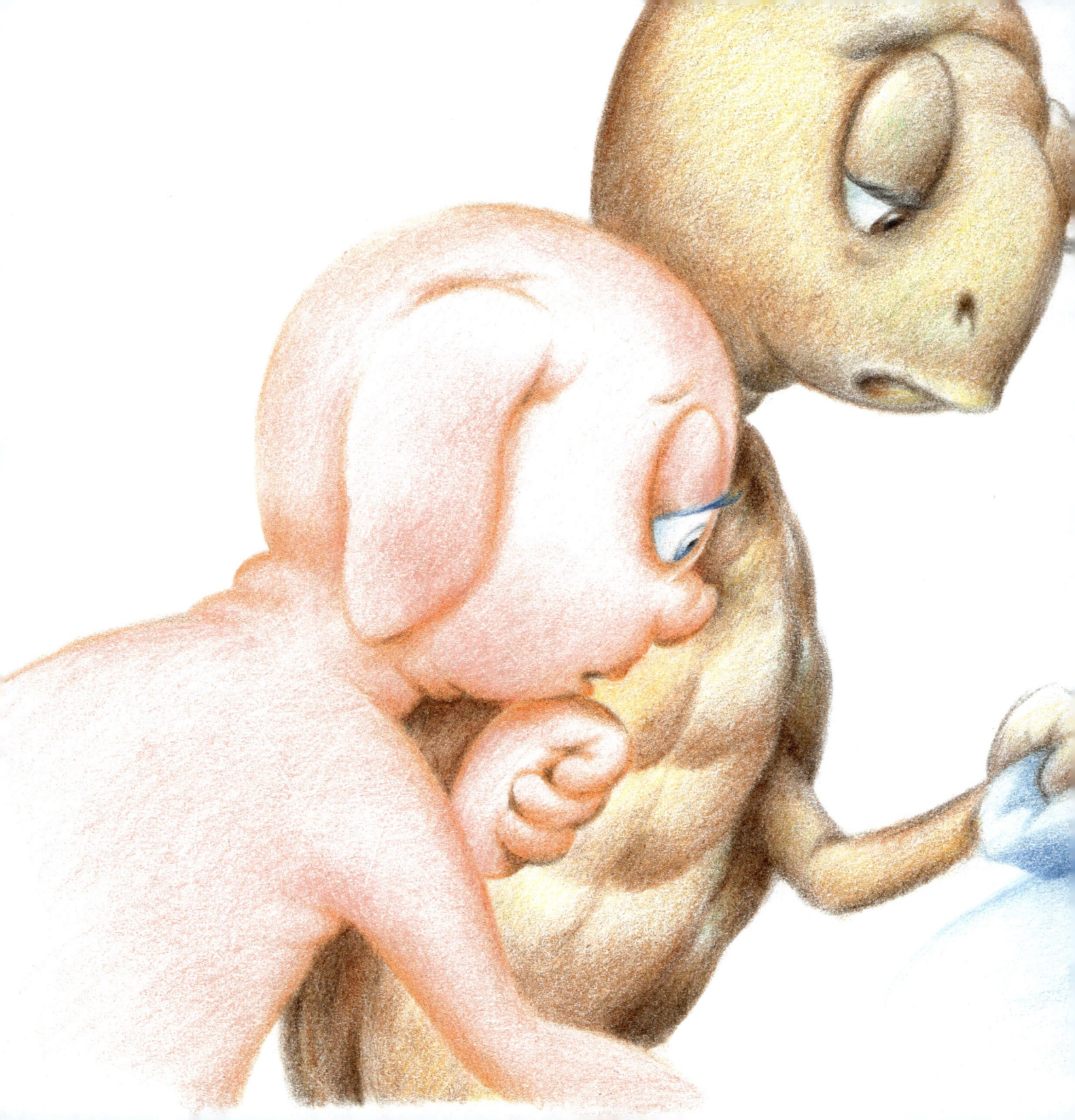

"Oh my! What's wrong with Peggy?" asks Mama Pig.

Papa Turtle spots Peggy Piggle hiding under her blanket.

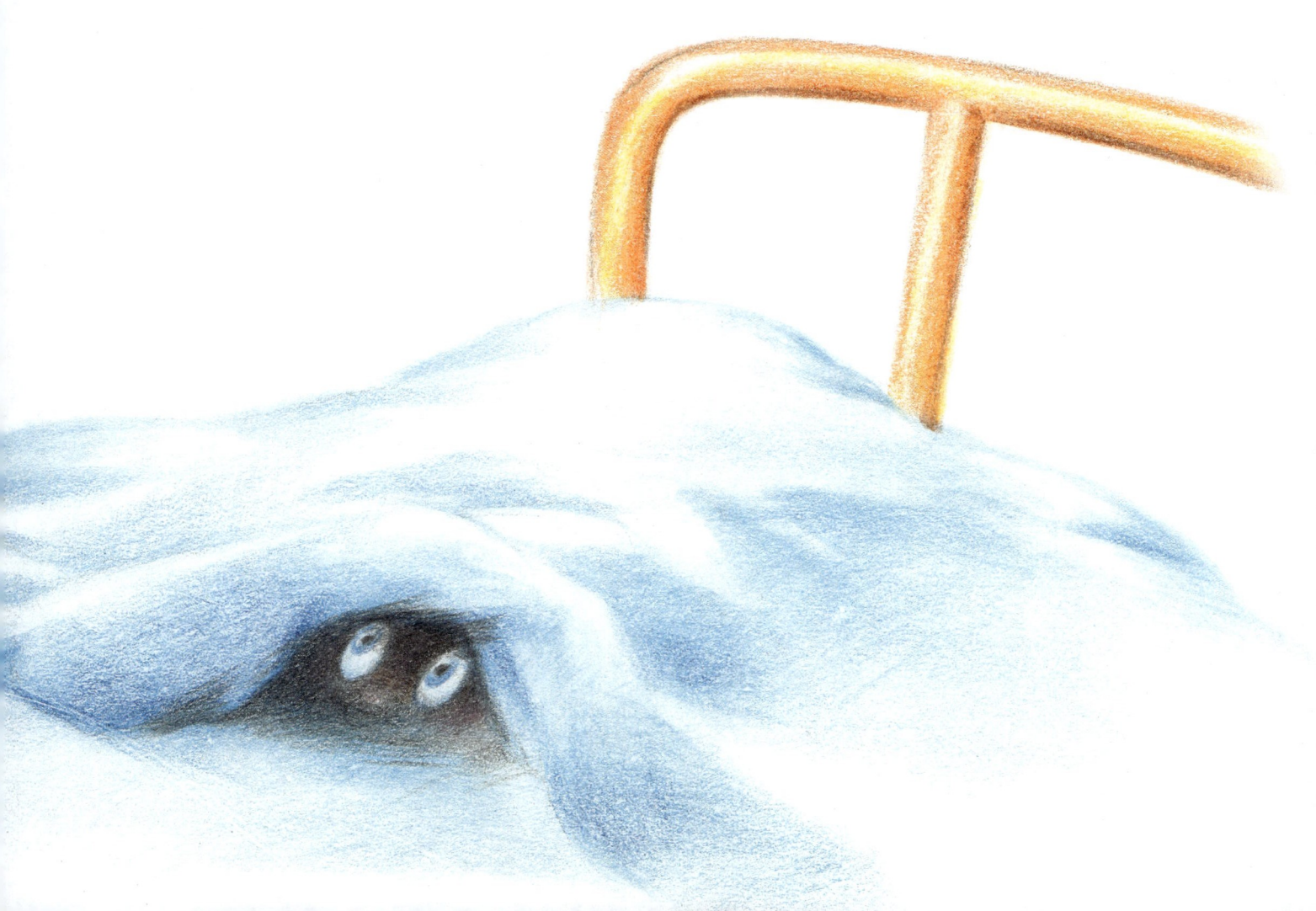

"Peggy, are you okay?" asks Papa Turtle. He lifts up the blanket, but she is still hiding in her shell.

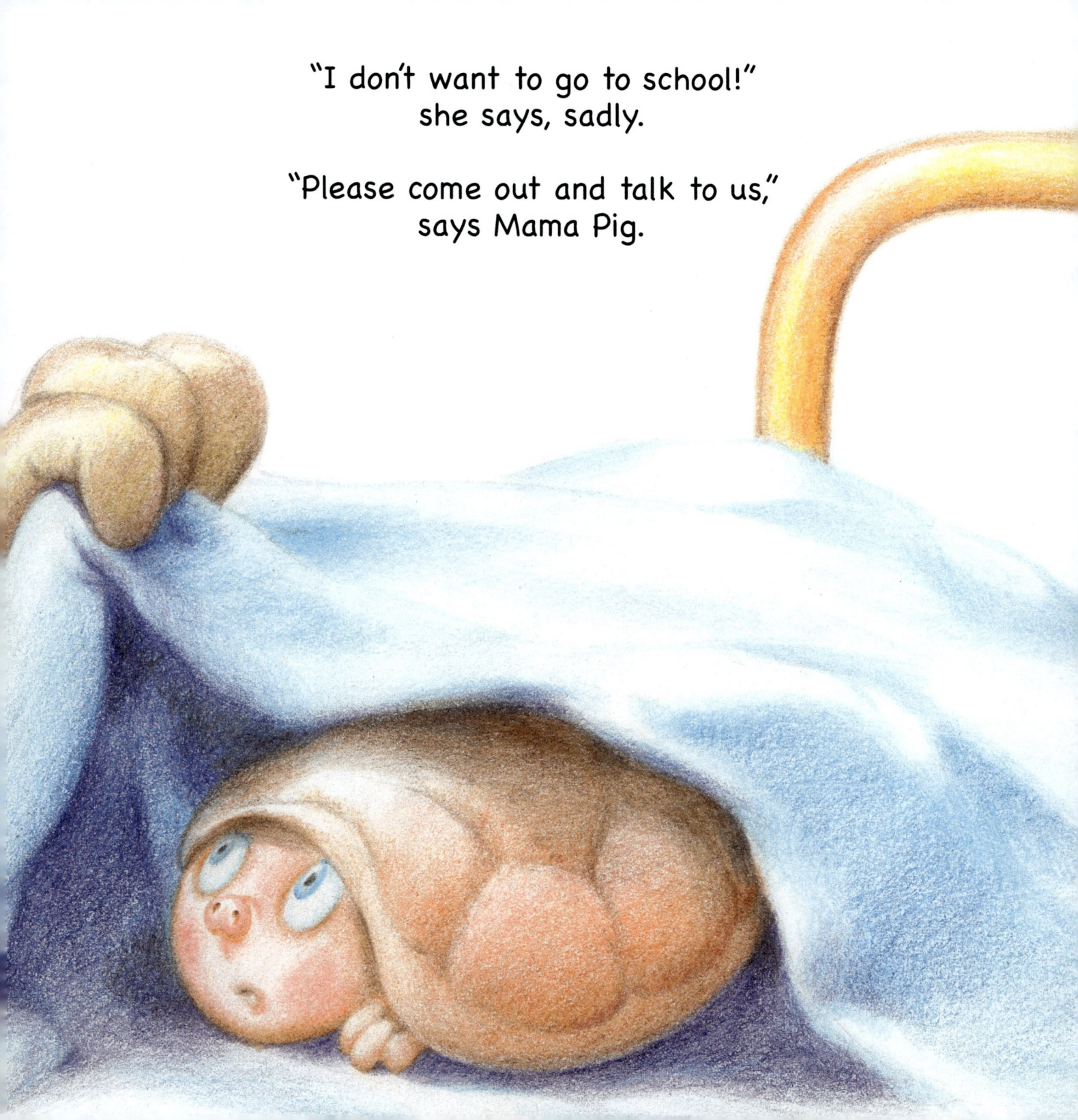

"I don't want to go to school!" she says, sadly.

"Please come out and talk to us," says Mama Pig.

Peggy Piggle creeps out of her shell.

"I don't know anyone at this new school," she whispers. "What if everyone thinks I'm different?"

Mama Pig looks down at Peggy Piggle.

"What is different about each of us makes us special, you will see."

"OK, Mama," says Peggy Piggle. "I guess I feel better, but I'm nervous."

Peggy Piggle climbs onto the school bus. She sits at the front, but looks behind at the others riding on the bus. Everyone looks different.
"Maybe Mama was right. It's not just me that is different," Peggy thinks.

Still nervous, Peggy Piggle tiptoes into the school yard. She is not used to being around so many others. Peggy Piggle is surrounded by animals and she does not know where to go.

She backs away and bumps into someone.

"Hi! Can I help?" asks Bobby Bearilla, peering down at her.

He is SO big!

Poor Peggy Piggle pops back into her shell, only her sad eyes peeking out. Bobby Bearilla, Tammy and Tommy Touguin, and Joey Koalaby circle around her.

Bobby Bearilla peeks into her shell.
"Are you okay?" he asks. "I didn't mean to scare you.
We are all friends here. You are safe." The others nod.
Peggy Piggle sees their smiling faces from inside her
shell and decides to come out.

Bobby Bearilla is first to introduce himself.
"Hi, I'm Bobby, it's nice to meet you."
"Hello, we are the twins, Tammy and Tommy,"
the two Touguins chatter.
"I'm Joey, it's nice to meet you!" giggles the Koalaby,
and he wiggles excitedly.

Peggy Piggle starts to feel happy about meeting new friends.
"Hi, my name is Peggy, and I'm new here," she mumbles, shyly. Olly Otver and Lucy Llapaca reply, "Welcome to the group!" Sally Skunny wiggles her ears and Zoey Ziraffe waves her tail.

Peggy Piggle walks to class with her new friends, but she doesn't watch where she is going.

Oh no! Peggy Piggle accidentally steps on someone's tail.

"OW! MEOW!" Sprinky, a big bad cat, arches his back and hisses at Peggy.

ZIP! Poor Peggy Piggle slips back into her shell.
Bobby Bearilla and the others feel so sorry for her.

"Sprinky," growls Bobby, "you are scaring Peggy. She didn't mean to step on your tail. It was an accident."

"Well, she'd better watch out. Next time I won't be so nice," Sprinky snarls, and strolls away.

"You can come out now, Peggy, he's gone," says Bobby. She moves slowly out of her shell.

"Who was that?" she asks. "He's very scary."

"That's Sprinky, and don't worry. He's not so huffy once you get to know him. Mostly fluffy," chuckles Joey.

Peggy Piggle and Bobby Bearilla find a seat in class, right next to each other. Peggy leans over to Bobby.

"Thank you for helping me today," she smiles.

"That's what friends are for," grins Bobby, and he gives her a high-five.

The rest of the school day is fun.

Maggy Moorse is a fabulous teacher, leading everyone in lessons, songs and games.

Peggy Piggle is careful to give Sprinky plenty of space, but she leaves her lunch cookie on his mat.

Peggy feels so happy, as she skips to the bus with Bobby Bearilla.

On the ride home, she is surrounded by her new friends. Everyone IS different! She waves to everyone as she gets off at her stop.

As the bus pulls away, Sprinky slowly waves his tail at her through the window.

With a gigantic smile, Peggy Piggle hurries into the house. Mama Pig and Papa Turtle are excited to hear all about her first day at school.

"I met so many great new friends today!" exclaimed Peggy Piggle. "Perhaps even a cat!"

"Everyone IS different, just like me," says Peggy with a big smile.

"We knew you would enjoy your self and make new friends" said Papa Turtle.

Peggy Piggle hugs Mama Pig.

"You were right, Mama. What is different about each of us is what makes us special ... and I feel special."

Made in United States
Orlando, FL
19 August 2024